The Mozart Starter

The Mozart Starter

Exploring the Universe
of
Mozart's Music

Bruce Cooper Clarke

Foreword
by Christopher Hogwood

CREDITS

Cover portrait: *Wolfgang Amadé Mozart* by Barbara Krafft,
from the collection of the Gesellschaft der Musikfreunde
in Vienna, Austria.

Page 8: *W. A. Mozart on the Piano.* Unfinished portrait by
Joseph Lange, from the collection at the Mozarteum in
Salzburg.

All other illustrations are original pen and ink drawings by
Belinda Belding.

Cover design by Digital Media, Bloomington, Illinois.

LIBRARY OF CONGRESS CATALOGING-IN-PUBLICATION DATA:

Clarke, Bruce Cooper, 1926-
  The Mozart starter : exploring the universe of
  Mozart's music / by Bruce Cooper Clarke ; with a
  foreword by Christopher Hogwood.
          p.   cm.
  Includes bibliographical references and index.
  ISBN 0-936741-06-6
  1. Mozart, Wolfgang Amadeus, 1756-1791.
  2. Composers--Austria--Biography. I. Title.
  ML410.M9C4477 1995
  780' .92--dc20   95-1396
                                               CIP
                                               MN

MEDI-ED PRESS
Constitution Place, Suite A
716 East Empire Street
Bloomington, Illinois 61701
1-800-500-8205

Contents

For Bessie

Mozart am Klavier by Joseph Lange

Foreword

As a hater of crossword puzzles and all that mind-bending word-splitting, I am surprised that there is one anagram that appeals to me: Mozart becomes

MR A TO Z

Not only is it neat,—it's true; he worked in every form and style available to him, and invented a few that weren't. No wonder that although this anagram may delight the initiated, it's a deterrent to a new enthusiast. The area is too large, too bewildering, too unmapped—but now

"Hats off, gentlemen! A Starter!"

If you've found Köchel numbers kaleidoscopic, and Cassations confusing, then start with what you already enjoy and work onwards.

This compact companion views the panorama with enthusiasm, and, like a good tourist guide, draws your view from the landmark you know to the gem you had never noticed.   And if on the journey you feel like crossing swords over a few topics (I want a word on the *Requiem* and *opera seria*), remember that a starter ignites as well as invigorates — from A TO Z.

Christopher Hogwood
Cambridge, November 1994

Preface

You, Dear Reader, need music; it is a biological necessity. The fact that you are reading these words shows that you sense this need and are responding to it. Just why human beings have a biological need for music and, indeed, just what music is, are questions for which there are no definitive answers, at least not yet. But the need is there.

Out of this need, men and women since the dawn of time have sought to express themselves in music. Those most gifted have devoted their lives to its composing. Out of the literally thousands of composers over the millennia, a relatively small number have been able to write music so universally compelling that it transcends boundaries, nationalities, and time. Mozart is one of the few.

There is a unique quality to the music Mozart wrote. More so than with almost any other composer, his music can be heard, appreciated, and enjoyed at several levels.

We are usually struck at first by its joyousness and lightness of being, the sheer delight of the music-maker in making music. Yet at the same time, we can feel— subliminally—a primal sob, a kind of cosmic catch in the throat, for the beauty and fleetingness of life. And all this is done with extraordinary mastery of the art of composing and with impeccable self-control. There is no self-pity in Mozart.

In a brilliant essay on Mozart at the time of the bicentenary of his death, the German historian Michael Stürmer closed with these words:

> Being the artist he was, Mozart had discerned the tectonic strains and tensions of his times and creatively set them to music as though dictated from within. And thus it happens, if we choose, we can hear in his music nothing but the joy and poetic fancy that moved him. But it also happens that we can sense...his anguish, as the lamps of his epoch flickered and died one by one and, with them, his own life as well.

Mozart's music captivates the intellect and delights the senses. At least that has been my experience, and I hope it may be yours too. To that end, this little book is dedicated.

Bruce Cooper Clarke

Mozart's Music

In his thirty years or so as an active composer, Wolfgang Amadé Mozart created a vast musical universe. A remarkable amount of it has survived the interceding two centuries. And a remarkable amount of it is of transcendent relevance and interest to us today and a source of great pleasure.

Mozart's music is ubiquitous. As the 20th century turns into the 21st, no symphony season without it is imaginable; no opera company worthy of the name can afford to ignore him; no would-be virtuoso soloist— whether on the piano, the violin, the clarinet, horn, flute or bassoon—can fail to include a Mozart concerto in his or her repertory.

All of us know some of Mozart's greatest music—the Jupiter symphony, the "Elvira Madigan" piano concerto (or at least its andante second movement), the overtures to *Figaro* and *The Magic Flute*, the rondo *alla Turca* from the A-major piano sonata, and, last but certainly not least, the Requiem. But few of us know the farther reaches of Mozart's universe.

In days gone by, that was understandable: concert programmers chose from a relatively narrow range of Mozart's compositions and scheduled the same pieces— *Eine kleine Nachtmusik*, the late G-minor symphony, and the D-minor piano concerto—over and over again. And the recording companies—pre-CD—were seldom much more enterprising.

But now, thanks in part to the spur given by the 200th anniversary of Mozart's death in 1991, virtually the entire Mozart oeuvre has been recorded. It is there, waiting to be discovered and enjoyed. All we need is a little bit of help from our friends to get started on a voyage through this universe of sound.

This little book is intended to do just that: to help you move beyond what you already know into less familiar— but no less enjoyable and rewarding—realms of Mozart's music. To that end, I have divided Mozart's music into ten categories and offer my suggestions on where you might go next in each of them. They are summarized in the *Checklist* at the end.

You will want to know much more about Mozart and his music than I can tell you here. There is almost no end to the number and kind of books written about him. In a section at the back, I have listed a short selection of recent books I think you would enjoy reading. Most of them are available in paperback and all of them reflect the wealth of recent Mozart research.

In this book, Mozart's works are identified primarily by their so-called Köchel numbers (Ludwig von Köchel having published the first comprehensive chronological catalog of Mozart's music in 1862). Over the years, the Köchel numbering system has become a bit chaotic as new research has made more accurate dating of the works possible. But if you are looking for a work and you find that it has two or more numbers, usually one of them will be the number given here.

The Symphonies

The distance traveled by Mozart from his first symphony to his last, over a period of some twenty-four years, is greater than the distance traveled from Mozart's last symphony to the present. For much of this journey, Joseph Haydn was Mozart's great influence and example; at the end, it was just the reverse.

You probably already know the much-programmed last five symphonies:

C-major, No. 36 ("Linz") K. 425; D-major, No. 38 ("Prague") K. 504; E-flat, No. 39 K. 543; G-minor No. 40 K. 550; and C-major, No. 41 ("Jupiter") K. 551.

In addition to these five, there are some forty-five other symphonies to choose from, tracing Mozart's development as a symphonist and as a composer from the time he was eight years old to when he was thirty-two. Five suggestions:

—F-major, No. 6 K. 43: one of Mozart's first symphonies, and probably the first to have four movements; lilting first and last movements and a serene second movement with flutes and muted violins; few eleven-year-olds have done better.

—D-minor K. 118: representative of numerous Mozart symphonies derived from overtures to operas and oratorios; in three movements, normally played without a break; his first symphony in the minor, a harbinger of things to come.

—E-flat, No. 19 K. 132: written five years after K. 43, Mozart is older and more ready to experiment and the orchestra is larger (four horns instead of two); a symphony in changing moods with an introspective second movement unlike any written up to the year 1772.

—G-minor, No. 25 K. 183: the so-called "little" G-minor (No. 40 K. 550 being the "great" G-minor), composed in 1773; perhaps already known to you from the film "Amadeus";

properly performed, a thrilling work, and an important milestone on the way to the concert supremacy of the symphony.

—B-flat, No. 33 K. 319: written originally in Salzburg in 1779 in three movements, Mozart added a minuet and trio when he performed it after moving to Vienna; in its orchestration and compositional subtlety, another step nearer to the evolution of Mozart's symphonic conception evident in the last five.

The Piano Concertos

Whereas the development of the symphonic form was essentially the joint accomplishment of Joseph Haydn and Mozart, the elevation of the piano concerto into "the most highly organized of all purely instrumental forms" (as the English musicologist Arthur Hutchings puts it) is almost entirely the work of Mozart.

He was twelve years old and living in Salzburg when he first began experimenting with how to write a piano concerto. By the time he had composed the last, K. 595, in Vienna in 1791, he had written twenty-seven altogether. Twelve of the finest—from K. 449 to K. 503

and those with Köchel numbers in between—were composed in a span of some three years from 1784 to 1786.

The three piano concertos most frequently programmed tend to be the C-major, No. 21 K. 467 (with its gravity-defying "Elvira Madigan" second movement) and the two darkly romantic minor-key concertos, D-minor, No. 20 K. 466 and C-minor, No. 24 K. 491. If you don't know them, start here.

You can choose Mozart piano concertos from the shelf with your eyes closed and not go wrong; this even applies to the very earliest ones which are youthful arrangements of other composers' piano works in concerto form. But five suggestions, nonetheless:

    —D-major, No. 5 K. 175: Mozart's first piano concerto entirely of his own composition, written in Salzburg when he was seventeen; an ingratiating and altogether joyous work.

    —E-flat, No. 9 K. 271: for American musicologist Charles Rosen, "perhaps the first unequivocal masterpiece in a classical style"; twenty-one-year-old Mozart in a mellow, experimental mood, with a minor-key second movement and a slow section suddenly appearing in the last movement.

—F-major, No. 19 K. 459: Mozart is twenty-eight, making his way in Vienna, and in the midst of a remarkably productive period; he is much in demand as a performer and to help meet the demand, he wrote this radiant and graceful concerto.

—A-major, No 23 K. 488: One of Mozart's most personal works with an almost improvisatory feel, full of unexpected touches, and a deeply meditative second movement in the unusual key of F-sharp minor.

—C-major, No. 25 K. 503: Written in December 1786 just before the Prague symphony, this remarkable concerto brought a temporary end to Mozart's work in this form; it has a first movement of regal splendor, a quirky second movement that I find oddly satisfying, and a splendid, constantly shifting last movement.

Concertos for Strings and Winds

Being the consummate musician he was, Mozart also wrote concertos for instruments other than the piano. This was something that happened at intervals from the time of his first concerto (for the violin in B-flat K. 207) in 1773 to the very end of his life (the clarinet concerto in A-major K. 622, finished in October 1791). He even wrote concertos for two or more instruments, as we shall see below.

Let me assume that you already know the clarinet concerto, which gained some currency in recent years from its use in the film "Out of Africa," and the horn concertos which, because of their endless flow of melody, find themselves programmed whenever an even halfway capable horn soloist turns up. In recordings, the four horn concertos often travel together; the K numbers are: 412, 417, 447, and 495. If these concertos are not in your collection, then this is a good place to start. The clarinet concerto in particular is the greatest of its kind.

As for where to go next, let me suggest:

—The violin concertos. There are five: B-flat, No. 1 K. 207; D-major, No. 2 K. 211; G-major, No. 3 K. 216; D-major, No. 4 K. 218; A-major, No. 5 ("Turkish") K. 219. Start with the G-major, No. 3 K. 216—it is a grand work, every movement a jewel—then you can go in either direction to the others.

—The sinfonia concertante for violin and viola in E-flat K. 364. This concerto for two instruments is one the glories of Western music. In it, Mozart brilliantly solved the problem of the balance between the two solo string instruments and the orchestra. The second movement is one of the most deeply felt he ever wrote.

Chamber Music for Strings

Chamber music, it has been said, is not composed to be heard but to be played, for the performers are the audience. And this may be one reason why it is not easy to write good chamber music: each part stands out and the performing audience is critical. Mozart— whose string quartets and quintets reach across his entire composing life—once said he found writing them "hard work." But it was worth it; the last ten of his more than twenty string quartets are among his greatest works.

If you're already into string quartets and other chamber music, then you probably know substantial parts of the Mozart oeuvre and can skip this section. But, if you're not, then some suggestions follow:

—You might start with the three so-called divertimentos for string quartet, D-major K. 136, B-flat K. 137, and F-major K. 138. These delightful works, written when Mozart was fifteen or sixteen, are also often performed by small orchestral ensembles instead of just one-on-a-part.

—Mozart's "hard work" remark applied to the task of writing the six string quartets he dedicated to Haydn, a project that took over two years. These quartets—G-major, No. 14 K. 387; D-minor, No. 15 K. 421; E-flat, No. 16 K. 428; B-flat, No. 17 ("Hunt") K. 458; A-major, No. 18 K. 464; and C-major, No. 19 ("Dissonance") K. 465—are something of a self-contained galactic system in the Mozart universe; once you learn them, they will be with you forever.

—Mozart wrote six string quintets (with a second viola added to the usual two violins, viola, and cello). A pair with extraordinary beauty and contrast are the two quintets, in C-major K. 515 and in G-minor K. 516, composed in 1787, not long after the Prague symphony and the majestic C-major piano concerto K. 503, mentioned above.

—Finally, let me suggest a remarkable work, composed a year later—a trio for violin, viola and cello in E-flat K. 563, which contains six movements and which Mozart chose to call a "divertimento." A fascinating composition.

Other Chamber Music

Chamber music, with one person on a part, is written for all kinds of instruments and in many combinations. This sort of music sold well in the 18th century and Mozart wrote lots of it to help out his cash flow: pieces for violin and piano, or for piano and two or more instruments, or for combinations of strings and winds. Five suggestions out of literally dozens to choose from:

> —Flute quartet in D-major, No. 1 K. 285; a youthful work for flute, violin, viola, and cello, written in three movements, with a meltingly lovely adagio second movement that leads directly into the third.

·   —Quintet in E-flat K. 452 for piano, oboe, clarinet, bassoon and horn. A product of Mozart's joy in experimentation, the listing of the instruments alone tells you that this is something unusual; indeed, this was probably the first piano and wind quintet ever written: a challenging musical problem, a marvelous musical solution.

—Sonata in B-flat K. 454 for violin and piano, written in Vienna in 1784 for a joint performance with the Italian violin virtuosa, Regina Strinassachi. It is a complex composition rich in chromaticism, with an unusual largo introduction to the first movement.

—Piano quartet in G-minor K. 478. Not Mozart's most immediately ingratiating work, it has an austere, autumnal quality, realized most completely perhaps in the beautiful andante second movement.

—Clarinet quintet in A-major K. 581. The chamber music precursor of the clarinet concerto, written for the same soloist some two years before. Broadly conceived in four movements, a lustrous and deeply satisfying work.

Music for the Piano

As a performer, Mozart was primarily a pianist (although his father thought it a shame he didn't apply himself more to the violin). And his Wunderkind reputation was established more by his precociousness as a pianist than as a composer. It is not surprising, then, that Mozart the composer worked all his life for Mozart the pianist (including his older sister, also a formidable piano soloist) and that there are over a hundred works, long and short, in a variety of forms, for solo piano (and for two pianos, and even for two persons at one piano).

Some suggestions as to where to start into Mozart's piano literature:

—The so-called "Opus 4" sonatas: C-major K. 309, D-major K. 311, and A-minor K. 310. Written in 1777 and 1778, they show Mozart reaching for new expressive possibilities within the piano sonata form. The A-minor sonata was composed in Paris after his mother unexpectedly died there, a work full of bitterness, resignation, and resolution.

—A second group of sonatas was composed some five years later: C-major K. 330, A-major K. 331, F-major K. 332, and B-flat K. 333. Large-scale, often entertaining works, probably written primarily to display the composer's pianistic talents in concert. If you're looking for the *alla Turca* movement, it is number three in K. 331.

—Mozart wrote numerous smaller, separate works for piano—minuets, marches, adagios and fantasias—works that often have the feel of the master in a meditative mood idly improvising at the piano. Do find his Adagio in B-minor K. 540 for one of the greatest compositions. Another is the Fantasia in C-minor K. 475, written and published as an introduction to the C-minor Sonata K. 457; when played together, thirty minutes of glorious music.

—For an example of Mozart composing for two pianos, seek out a performance of his Sonata in D-major K. 448, 18th century music-making at its best.

Divertimentos and Serenades—
Orchestral and Chamber Music

Here is a wealth of music written in forms called serenades (or, very early, cassations) and divertimentos by Mozart. They are generally broadly conceived works in multiple movements. With few exceptions, they were all written in Salzburg for specific social occasions. Roughly speaking, the serenades were written for outdoor performance and the divertimentos for indoors as chamber works. They often open and sometimes close with a march. On several occasions, Mozart later drew on a multi-movement serenade to create a four-movement symphony.

Unquestionably, the best known Mozart work in this
genre is the one Mozart called "Eine kleine NachtMusik"
when he noted it down in his catalog of compositions
on 10 August 1787 (it ultimately received the Köchel
number of 525). There it was listed as having five
movements; the original second movement has been
lost and only four have come down to us.

These so-called occasional pieces contain much music
of high spirits and tender sentiment. They are a treasure
trove waiting to be discovered. Here are some places
to start:

　　—Serenade in D-major ("Andretter") K. 185. An
　　early orchestral serenade composed in 1773, it
　　contains (as others did as well) what amounts
　　to an abbreviated violin concerto in the second
　　and third movements, giving the first violinist
　　a chance to rise and shine.

　　—Serenade in D-major ("Haffner") K. 250.
　　While America was declaring independence in
　　July 1776, Mozart in Salzburg was writing this
　　imposing orchestral serenade, with its march
　　and eight movements, to celebrate a marriage
　　in the Haffner family. It begins with an
　　ambitiously symphonic first movement,
　　followed by an internal three-movement violin
　　concerto of great beauty, before returning to
　　its symphonic orientation.

—Serenade in D-major ("Posthorn") K. 320. This is the last of the orchestral serenades composed in Salzburg, in 1779, and for many, the greatest. There is no embedded violin concerto here; rather, the "concertino" in the third and fourth movements is given over to pairs of flutes, oboes and bassoons. The posthorn solo which gives the piece its name shows up towards the end, in the second trio of the second minuet.

—Serenade in B-flat ("gran Partita") K. 361. Although there is disagreement over exactly when Mozart wrote this extraordinary serenade for wind instruments (was it 1781-82 or 1783-84?), everyone agrees it is the *ne plus ultra* in the realm of *Harmoniemusik*, that is, music written for wind instrument ensembles. Mozart combines pairs of oboes, clarinets, basset-horns and bassoons with two pairs of horns and a double-bass, thirteen instruments in all, for seven diverse, spacious movements.

—Serenade in C-minor K. 388. Another of Mozart's Vienna wind serenades, this one for the more usual combination of pairs of oboes, clarinets, horns and bassoons. Unusual, however, is the structure in only four movements and, most especially, the minor key, which gives this wind serenade, a category

more commonly associated with genial
company and a convivial glass of wine, an
enduring seriousness of tone and purpose.
Demanding music to perform well, rewarding
music to hear.

Music for the Church

Mozart's substantial body of sacred works is, with notable exceptions, music largely written in and for Salzburg; once he too had declared his independence (from the Church's employ) and settled in Vienna in 1781, he composed relatively little for liturgical use, although that little contains some of his greatest music.

Leaving aside the Requiem for the moment, let me assume that you are familiar with the early (1773) motet for soprano and orchestra, "*Exsultate, jubilate*" K. 165, with the two large, late-Salzburg masses—Missa in C-major K. 317 ("Coronation") and the Missa solemnis in C-major K. 337—and with that little jewel of a motet, *"Ave verum corpus"* K. 618, wrought in June of his last year.

Four suggestions out of many to choose from:

—The Missa solemnis in C-minor K. 139, known as the *Waisenhausmesse* because it was written (we think) for the consecration of a new Orphanage Church in Vienna in 1768. The work is such a brilliant accomplishment that, to this day, people have difficulty believing Mozart could have been only twelve years old when he composed it.

—The concert oratorio, *La Betulia liberata* K. 118, written during one of Mozart's Italian trips when he was fifteen. From the overture came a D-minor symphony, as mentioned above. The strong story-line—featuring a contralto as heroine who saves the besieged city of Betulia by seducing the besieger and cutting off his head (all of this long before Richard Strauss ever thought of Salomé)— results in strong music, with the chorus accorded a prominent role.

—The set of vespers, *Vesperae solennes de confessore* K. 339, for soloists, chorus and orchestra, composed as part of his churchly duties in Salzburg in 1780. In setting the psalms,

Mozart ranges freely through a variety of musical styles before reaching the *Laudate Dominum* with a soprano solo floating over a soft choral texture (which one writer found "enchanting and poetic" and led him to suspect Mozart of being "completely unconcerned with anything churchly" at the time of its composing).

—And with that, we are landed at the Missa in C-minor K. 427. This magnificent work was intended for liturgical use in the church and, even though incomplete, had its first performance in St. Peter's in Salzburg in 1783 when Mozart and his bride were visiting there; Constanze sang one of the soprano parts. Because Mozart never got around to finishing it, however, it has tended to become primarily a concert piece. As such, it is an enduring reminder of Mozart's genius, a musical feast and balm for the troubled soul.

Here let me mention two Mozart works associated with death and grief and mourning, two compelling works that you should have in your collection:

—The one is the dirge K. 477, known as the Masonic Funeral Music, a short, indescribably intense elegiac work in C-minor which, in a powerful metaphor of grief assuaged and peace attained, ends on a C-major chord.

—The other you know—the Requiem. Because Mozart did not live to finish it and it was brought to liturgical completeness by others in his circle, principally his musical assistant Süssmayr, people have been tinkering with it ever since. Among the many editions available, a recent one presumes to purify the Requiem as we know it of alleged alien influences (especially Süssmayr's); this jettisons much music which Mozart may have shaped even if he never orchestrated it, effectively reduces its performance time from some 60 minutes to about 43 minutes, and negates its liturgical validity; be warned.

Music for the Voice
Concert Arias, Songs, Canons

If we simply add up all the pieces Mozart wrote for voice (leaving out the operas), it looks like this: solo songs with piano, more than thirty; vocal ensembles, eight; canons of all kinds, thirty-plus; concert arias and scenes for voice and orchestra—for soprano (over thirty), for alto (one), for tenor (nine), and for bass (eight). Altogether, more than one hundred twenty, from his earliest days to his last.

Probably the best known of his songs is *Das Veilchen* K. 476. But there are many others to recommend as starting points in learning Mozart's lieder: *Das Lied der*

Trennung K. 519; *Als Luise die Briefe ihres ungetreuen Liebhabers verbrannte* K. 520; *Abendempfindung an Laura* K. 523; and *An Chloe* K. 524.

That Mozart wrote some fifty independent and concert arias and scenes (that is, an aria with an introductory recitative) is a reflection of the music business at the time. For one thing, it was not uncommon for one composer to write arias at the behest of a singer for inclusion in another composer's opera, and Mozart wrote several of these. For another, concert programs routinely included one or two solo performances by singers in addition to the purely orchestral works, and Mozart was in demand as a composer for these kinds of concert pieces.

Choosing from the broad palette of Mozart's compositions in this form, let me suggest:

   —"*Vorrei spiegarvi, oh Dio*" K. 418: Mozart prided himself on his ability to compose arias tailor-made to give full display to the vocal abilities of the recipient. If this demanding and beautiful aria faithfully mirrors the voice of Aloisia Lange, his sister-in-law, for whom it was written to sing in an opera by Anfossi, then she must have been a singer of great range and talent indeed.

   —"*Per pietà, non ricercate*" K. 420: written in June 1783 at the same time as K. 418 and for inclusion in the same Anfossi opera, but for

Music for the Piano

As a performer, Mozart was primarily a pianist (although his father thought it a shame he didn't apply himself more to the violin). And his Wunderkind reputation was established more by his precociousness as a pianist than as a composer. It is not surprising, then, that Mozart the composer worked all his life for Mozart the pianist (including his older sister, also a formidable piano soloist) and that there are over a hundred works, long and short, in a variety of forms, for solo piano (and for two pianos, and even for two persons at one piano).

Some suggestions as to where to start into Mozart's piano literature:

—The so-called "Opus 4" sonatas: C-major K. 309, D-major K. 311, and A-minor K. 310. Written in 1777 and 1778, they show Mozart reaching for new expressive possibilities within the piano sonata form. The A-minor sonata was composed in Paris after his mother unexpectedly died there, a work full of bitterness, resignation, and resolution.

—A second group of sonatas was composed some five years later: C-major K. 330, A-major K. 331, F-major K. 332, and B-flat K. 333. Large-scale, often entertaining works, probably written primarily to display the composer's pianistic talents in concert. If you're looking for the *alla Turca* movement, it is number three in K. 331.

—Mozart wrote numerous smaller, separate works for piano—minuets, marches, adagios and fantasias—works that often have the feel of the master in a meditative mood idly improvising at the piano. Do find his Adagio in B-minor K. 540 for one of the greatest compositions. Another is the Fantasia in C-minor K. 475, written and published as an introduction to the C-minor Sonata K. 457; when played together, thirty minutes of glorious music.

the tenor Johann Valentin Adamberger (who later decided not to use it, much to Mozart's disgust).

—"*Ch'io mi scordi di te?...Non temer, amato bene*" K. 505: Mozart entered this in his catalog on 27 December 1786, with the words, "<u>*Scena con Rondò*</u> *mit klavier solo. für Mad<u>selle</u> storace und mich*," and succeeded thereby in unleashing torrents of purple prose. To this day, persons claim to see—in these words and in this work—confirmation that Nancy Storace, the first Susanna in *Figaro*, and Mozart were lovers. Certainly the work, written for a farewell concert given by Storace, is one of intimacy and passion and the addition of an obbligato piano part for him to join her and the orchestra is both unusual and enchanting; one of the great Mozart concert arias. (And were they really lovers? Probably not.)

—"*Bella mia fiamma...Resta, o cara*" K. 528: another concert aria for soprano and orchestra, composed for the Bohemian singer Josepha Duschek, a longtime friend of the Mozart family, in Prague in 1787 while Mozart and Constanze were there for the premiere of *Don Giovanni*. A deeply felt evocation of leave-taking, as the singer laments, "*addio, addio, per sempre.*"

The Operas

Mozart the piano virtuoso and Mozart the composer were also Mozart the man of the theater. He loved to go to the theater, was widely read in dramatic literature, understood dramaturgy, and liked to be around theater people. More than anything else, he wanted to make it as a composer of opera. Salzburg had no opera theater, so he left; Vienna had several, so he stayed.

Mozart's first operatic work (*Apollo et Hyacinthus* K. 38) was performed in Salzburg when he was eleven years old; the last two—*Die Zauberflöte* (The Magic Flute) K. 620 and *La clemenza di Tito* (The Clemency of Titus) K. 621—in Vienna and Prague respectively in

the last months of his life. In between, he had written
some eighteen operatic works (not all of them to
completion) and changed forever the world's perception
of the potentialities of opera. A hundred years ago,
Bernard Shaw, in his role as music critic, wrote:

> Mozart's *Don Giovanni* has made all musical
> Europe conscious of the modern orchestra and
> of the perfect adaptability of music to the
> subtlest needs of the dramatist...After the finales
> in *Figaro* and *Don Giovanni*, the possibilities
> of the modern music drama lay bare.

Assumption: you know the overtures and much of the
music to *Le nozze di Figaro (The Marriage of Figaro)*
K. 492, *Don Giovanni* K. 527, and *The Magic Flute*, and
probably to *Die Entführung aus dem Serail (The
Abduction from the Seraglio)* K. 384 as well. If not,
start here.

It is tempting to write, "and then go on to all the others."
But I resist. Instead, let me suggest you go on to:

> —*Così fan tutte* K. 588, the third (along with
> *Figaro* and *Don Giovanni*) of the three great
> operas composed with Lorenzo Da Ponte as
> his inspired collaborating librettist. For many,
> *Così* is Mozart's most fascinating operatic
> achievement, a subtle, penetrating report from
> the front lines in the battle of the sexes, as
> modern as tomorrow.

Then turn to these three:

>—*Lucio Silla* K. 135, his seventh operatic work, written for performance in Milan in 1772, shortly before his seventeenth birthday.

>—*Idomeneo, rè di Creta* K. 366, composed for Munich at the end of 1780.

>—*La clemenza di Tito* K. 621, Mozart's last opera, commissioned for performance in Prague and taken up while he was in the middle of work on *The Magic Flute.*

These operas have this in common: they are all examples of the increasingly outmoded neoclassical *opera seria* form which Mozart, with his Da Ponte operas, did much to consign to history. Undaunted by the constraints of the arid *opera seria* form, Mozart filled each of them with vital, living music. I recommend *Idomeneo* especially.

The Mozart Starter Checklist

Works you probably already know:

- ❏   C-major, No. 36 ("Linz") K. 425
- ❏   D-major, No. 38 ("Prague") K. 504
- ❏   E-flat, No. 39 K. 543
- ❏   G-minor No. 40 K. 550
- ❏   C-major, No. 41 ("Jupiter") K. 551

Then go on to:

- ❏   F-major, No. 6 K. 43
- ❏   D-minor K. 118
- ❏   E-flat, No. 19 K. 132
- ❏   G-minor, No. 25 K. 183
- ❏   B-flat, No. 33 K. 319

Start with:

- ❏   C-major, No. 21 K. 467
- ❏   D-minor, No. 20 K. 466
- ❏   C-minor, No. 24 K. 491

Then go on to:

- ❏   D-major, No. 5 K. 175
- ❏   E-flat, No. 9 K. 271
- ❏   F-major, No. 19 K. 459
- ❏   A-major, No 23 K. 488
- ❏   C-major, No. 25 K. 503

Concertos for Strings and Winds   *page 25*

Start with:

- ❏ The clarinet concerto in A-major K. 622
- ❏ The four horn concertos K. 412, K. 417, K. 447 and K. 495

Then go on to:

The violin concertos:
- ❏ B-flat, No. 1 K. 207
- ❏ D-major, No. 2 K. 211
- ❏ G-major, No. 3 K. 216
- ❏ D-major, No. 4 K. 218
- ❏ A-major, No. 5 ("Turkish") K. 219
- ❏ The sinfonia concertante for violin and viola in E-flat K. 364

Chamber Music for Strings   *page 27*

Many persons are not into chamber music at all. Suggestions, then, for getting started with Mozart:

Three so-called divertimentos for string quartet:

- ❏ D-major K. 136
- ❏ B-flat K. 137
- ❏ F-major K. 138

The six string quartets dedicated to Haydn:

- ❏ G-major, No. 14 K. 387
- ❏ D-minor, No. 15 K. 421
- ❏ E-flat, No. 16 K. 428
- ❏ B-flat, No. 17 ("Hunt") K. 458
- ❏ A-major, No. 18 K. 464
- ❏ C-major, No. 19 ("Dissonance") K. 465

Two string quintets and a trio:

- ❑ C-major K. 515
- ❑ G-minor K. 516
- ❑ The trio for violin, viola and cello in E-flat K. 563

Other Chamber Music *page 31*

And for going elsewhere in Mozart's diverse chamber music:

- ❑ Flute quartet in D-major, No. 1 K. 285
- ❑ Quintet in E-flat K. 452 for piano, oboe, clarinet, bassoon and horn
- ❑ Sonata in B-flat K. 454 for violin and piano
- ❑ Piano quartet in G-minor K. 478
- ❑ Clarinet quintet in A-major K. 581

Music for the Piano *page 33*

Suggestions for becoming familiar with Mozart's piano music:

The so-called "Opus 4" sonatas:

- ❑ C-major K. 309
- ❑ D-major K. 311
- ❑ A-minor K. 310

A second, later group of sonatas:

- ❑ C-major K. 330
- ❑ A-major K. 331
- ❑ F-major K. 332
- ❑ B-flat K. 333

Other piano works:

- ❑ Sonata for two pianos in D-major K. 448
- ❑ Fantasia in C-minor K. 475
  and the companion C-minor Sonata K. 457
- ❑ Adagio in B-minor K. 540

*Divertimentos and Serenades—
Orchestral and Chamber Music* *page 37*

You already know:

- ❑ *Eine kleine Nachtmusik* K. 525

so go on to:

- ❑ Serenade in D-major ("Andretter") K. 185
- ❑ Serenade in D-major ("Haffner") K. 250
- ❑ Serenade in D-major ("Posthorn") K. 320
- ❑ Serenade in B-flat ("gran Partita") K. 361
- ❑ Serenade in C-minor K. 388

Music for the Church *page 41*

You probably already know:

- ❑ Motet for soprano and orchestra, *"Exsultate, jubilate"* K. 165
- ❑ Missa in C-major K. 317 ("Coronation")
- ❑ Missa solemnis in C-major K. 337
- ❑ Motet, *"Ave verum corpus"* K. 618
- ❑ Requiem K. 626

Go on to:

- ❑ Missa solemnis in C-minor K. 139
- ❑ Concert oratorio, *La Betulia liberata* K. 118
- ❑ Vespers: *Vesperae solennes de confessore* K. 339
- ❑ Missa in C-minor K. 427
- ❑ Masonic Funeral Music K. 477

Music for the Voice:
   Concert Arias, Songs, Canons   page 45

Suggestions for going into the songs beyond the familiar
❏ *Das Veilchen* K. 476:

   ❏ *Das Lied der Trennung* K. 519
   ❏ *Als Luise die Briefe ihres ungetreuen Liebhabers verbrannte* K. 520
   ❏ *Abendempfindung an Laura* K. 523
   ❏ *An Chloe* K. 524

Suggestions for learning Mozart's concert arias:

   ❏ For soprano, "*Vorrei spiegarvi, oh Dio*" K. 418
   ❏ For tenor, "*Per pietà, non ricercate*" K. 420
   ❏ For soprano with obbligato piano accompaniment, "*Ch'io mi scordi di te?...Non temer, amato bene*" K. 505
   ❏ For soprano, "*Bella mia fiamma...Resta, o cara*" K. 528

The Operas   page 49

You probably know:

   ❏ *Die Entführung aus dem Serail* K. 384
   ❏ *Le nozze di Figaro* K. 492
   ❏ *Don Giovanni* K. 527
   ❏ *Die Zauberflöte* K. 620

Go on to:

   ❏ *Lucio Silla* K. 135
   ❏ *Idomeneo, rè di Creta* K. 366
   ❏ *Così fan tutte* K. 588
   ❏ *La clemenza di Tito* K. 621

Suggested Readings on Mozart and His Music

By any measure, Mozart is one of the most important figures in the history of Western music. The literature addressed to him and his art is correspondingly immense. Out of literally thousands to choose from, here are twelve books I recommend. As with the music suggestions given before, these too are something of a "Starter." In the bibliographies of these books, you'll find many ideas about where to go next. (The listing is alphabetical by author.)

Wye Jamison Allanbrook, *Rhythmic Gesture in Mozart: Le nozze di Figaro and Don Giovanni* (University of Chicago Press; 1983).

> A deep but engagingly written look at the nature of Mozart's musical art and its historical context as illustrated by the author with two of Mozart's finest operas.

Volkmar Braunbehrens, *Mozart in Vienna, 1781-1791* (Grove Weidenfeld, New York: 1989; translated by Timothy Bell).

> This is the best recent biography of the composer. Its particular virtue is that, in giving us an objective and unadorned look at Mozart, it also helps us understand the times in which he lived and had to make his way.

Arthur Hutchings, *A Companion to Mozart's Piano Concertos* (Oxford University Press, New York; 1948, recently reprinted in paperback).

> This little book takes you by the hand through all of Mozart's piano concertos, from first to last. Hutchings's musicianship is profound, but his text is full of humor and delight; he loves every one of the concertos, even those he occasionally finds lacking.

Konrad Küster, *Mozart: A Musical Biography* (Oxford University Press, New York; 1995; translation by Mary Whittall).

> This book by one of Germany's new crop of Mozart researchers seeks to marry biographical detail with musical analysis. In doing so, it is necessarily selective with respect to both, but Küster has a judicious eye and made his selections well.

H. C. Robbins Landon, Ed., *The Mozart Compendium, A Guide to Mozart's Life and Music* (Thames and Hudson, London; 1990).

> Under Landon's magisterial direction, an international body of experts has produced a comprehensive review of everything you wanted to know about Mozart and were afraid to ask, from Mozart's family tree to his influence on later composers and on the history of music.

Robert D. Levin, *Who Wrote the Mozart Four-wind Concertante?* (Pendragon Press, New York; 1988).

It is not easy to combine musicology and a whodunit but the energetic and erudite American scholar and concert pianist has managed it quite well. A fascinating look at the abiding "authenticity" problem we face in connection with Mozart (and other great composers): was everything passed down with Mozart's name on it actually composed by him?

Anton Neumayr, *Music & Medicine: Haydn, Mozart, Beethoven, Schubert; Notes on Their Lives, Works, and Medical Histories* (Medi-Ed Press, Bloomington; 1994; translated by Bruce Cooper Clarke).

The medical history of Mozart and especially the circumstances of his death are a study in themselves. The author, a prominent Viennese doctor of internal medicine (and Mozarteum-trained musician), sifts through all the evidence, considers all the legends, and comes to an informed conclusion. "Amadeus" to the contrary notwithstanding, it wasn't psychoterror by Salieri.

Stanley Sadie, *The New Grove Mozart* (Macmillan Press, London; 1980; reprinted 1987).

This handy paperback was originally published as part of *The New Grove Dictionary of Music and Musicians*, of which the author is the editor. As befitting a work of encyclopedic character, it is long on dates and "known" facts and short on speculation and an author's personal idiosyncrasies, a welcome relief from many a Mozart book that tends to be just the reverse.

William Stafford, *Mozart's Death: A Corrective Survey of the Legends* (Macmillan Press, London; 1991).

Calling my attention to this book, Stanley Sadie said it embodies "some of the most sensible and rational thinking about Mozart of any recent work," and he is right. It is an exceptionally well-informed and well-reasoned survey of the sources for our knowledge of the circumstances of Mozart's life and death, and very well written besides.

Andrew Steptoe, *The Mozart-Da Ponte Operas* (Clarendon Press, Oxford; 1988).

The subtitle of this book—*The Cultural and Musical Background to* Le nozze di Figaro, Don Giovanni, *and* Così fan tutte—is the clue to this book's orientation, and to current emphases in Mozart research as well. It is not enough simply to oscillate endlessly around Mozart's navel; we must understand the historical forces and the social context of his times to be able to fashion an understanding of him and his music. Steptoe's book is a significant contribution to this end.

Alan Tyson, *Mozart: Studies of the Autograph Scores* (Harvard University Press; 1987).

> In the realm of Mozart research, Tyson stands out as the researcher's researcher. Do not be misled by the title: this book is anything but a dry-as-dust scholarly record devoted to learning more and more about less and less. After reading it, you will understand why Tyson is one of the most frequently quoted authors in contemporary Mozart literature.

Neal Zaslaw, *Mozart's Symphonies: Context, Performance Practice, Reception* (Clarendon Press, Oxford; 1989).

> There is no better discussion of Mozart's preoccupation with symphonic form, and all that that ultimately meant for the direction of Western music in the 200 years since, than this "study in music history" written by the Cornell professor of music.

Biographical Notes

Bruce Cooper Clarke

Bruce Cooper Clarke is a student of the music of the Viennese classical period and the author of numerous articles, reports, and reviews concerned principally with Mozart. Mr. Clarke is a graduate of Syracuse University and the American University (Washington, D.C.). He and his family live in the foothills of the Austrian Alps, about midway between Salzburg (where Mozart was born) and Vienna (where he died).

Christopher Hogwood

Christopher Hogwood, founder of the modern revival of The Academy of Ancient Music, is considered a pioneer in the field of "authentic" music making. He has a worldwide conducting schedule, has amassed a celebrated catalogue of recordings, including all of Mozart's symphonies, and enjoys a fine reputation as a harpsichordist and clavichord player .

The Artist

Belinda Belding, creator of the pen and ink sketches throughout *The Mozart Starter,* is an artist and a free-lance illustrator who resides in Lansing, Michigan. She has worked with many art forms and media, including oil pastels, pen and ink, watercolors, and precious and semiprecious metals.